RETURN TO MOSCOW

A SHORT STORY

JOHN SAGER

Library of Congress Control Number: 2024917392

ISBN: 979-8-3305-0230-1 (Paperback)
ISBN: 979-8-3303-5194-7 (Hardcover)

Printed in the USA by Book House Publishing
Bellingham, WA

— Also by John Sager —

A Tiffany Monday—an Unusual Love Story, West Bow Press, 2012

Joan's Gallery, 50 Years of Artistry by Joan Johnson Sager, Blurb, Inc. 2013

Uncovered—My Half-Century with the CIA, West Bow Press, 2013

Night Flight, A Novel, CreateSpace, 2013

Operation Night Hawk, A Novel, CreateSpace, 2014

Moscow at Midnight, A Novel, CreateSpace, 2014

The Jihadists' Revenge, A Novel, CreateSpace, 2014

Mole, A Novel, CreateSpace, 2015

Capital Crises, A Novel, CreateSpace, 2015

God's Listeners, An Anthology, CreateSpace, 2015

Crescent Blood, A Novel, CreateSpace, 2016

Sasha—From Stalin to Obama, a Biography, CreateSpace 2016

Shahnoza—Super Spy, A Novel, CreateSpace, 2016

Target Oahu, A Novel, CreateSpace, 2017

Aerosol, A Novel, CreateSpace, 2017

The Health Center, A Novel, CreateSpace, 2017

The Conservator, A Biography, CreateSpace, 2017

The Evil Alliance, A Novel, CreateSpace, 2018

Tehran Revisited, A Novel, Archway Publishers, 2019

St. Barnabas, A Novel, Inspiring Voices, 2019

The Caravan, A Novel, Outskirts Press, 2019

Senator McPherson, A Novel, Inspiring Voices, 2019

Meetings in Moscow, A Novel, Outskirts Press, 2019

Madam President, A Novel, Outskirts Press, 2019

Kiwi Country, A Novel, Outskirts Press, 2020

Inside Iran, A Novel, Outskirts Press, 2020

ONE

THE MOURNERS, TWENTY-EIGHT OF THEM, slowly filed out of McLean's Trinity Lutheran church entrance, shaking the pastor's hand as they did so. It had been a solemn service, more so because the parents had insisted on a closed casket. Even so, everyone knew what was in it, the embalmed remains of two-year-old Roberta Oxner.

Months earlier, their physician had told them that little Roberta had an incurable cancer, deep inside her brain and thus inoperable and, eventually, fatal. But knowing this didn't make it easier. Oxner and his wife Natasha had been comfortably settled in their two-year-old home in McLean, Virginia, not far from the CIA headquarters building.

Oxner had been called out of retirement and after visiting one of his former agency colleagues, he had been asked to shed his retirement, come back on duty, and return to Moscow as its Chief of Station.

Why?, he asked. The answer was what he might have expected: The current COS had been declared persona non grata by the Russian Office of Foreign Affairs, which claimed that Chief of

Station Michael Forrester had been observed talking to a Russian diplomat, the assumption being that the diplomat had been recruited by Forrester. The same old same old, "career management," Russian style.

"SWEETHEART, WE'VE BOTH BEEN THROUGH THIS before. Fortunately, our diplomatic passports are still valid although they need to be updated. Our liaison people can take care of that."

"What about our car, Robert? It's only a year old."

"You're right, Natasha, but Avis has a buy-back program. We'll lose a few hundred dollars, maybe more, but we can afford it."

"And our home?"

"Good question. But the agency has plenty of connections with real estate people here in northern Virginia; we'll have to rely on them to make it happen.

"'And one more thing. One of our friends at headquarters has already tasked the Travel Office to buy our tickets: First Class (no kidding) Dulles International non-stop to London's Heathrow and from there non-stop to Moscow's Sheremetovo. I figure about eighteen hours, but we can nap along the way."

Two

Oxner was wrong. Even at cruising altitude the Delta Dreamliner ran into strong headwinds and they arrived about an hour later than scheduled. At baggage control, Oxner used his iPhone and learned that his driver was waiting outside. "Thank the Good Lord for modern technology."

"So, Igor, I can tell you've been expecting us. What's new that we should know?"

"For one thing, Sir, everything in the embassy building is automated, something the State Department contracted for with IBM. Every door is automatically shut and can only be opened with this fob, one for you and one for your wife. It's the same with the elevators, even the embassy cafeteria in the basement.

"Your cover assignment, that of Special Assistant to the Ambassador, allows you to move about the building without having to use the fob. Same for Mrs. Oxner who, as I understand it, is coming aboard as your personal assistant. First time a woman has had that position but once the word gets around, everybody will understand."

"And housing?"

"Oh, yes. Your apartment is one of the largest in the building because the two of you are expected to do a lot of entertaining. And I learned yesterday that a Russian woman—Ekatarina Orlova is her name—will be on call to help with your entertaining any time it's required."

"A woman? Should I be worried, Robert?" "Not a chance, Natasha, she could be old enough to be your mother."

"What do you know about ambassador Jenkins. Tough, easy-going, what?"

"He's an amazing guy. Before coming here he served in London, Berlin and Madrid. So he speaks pretty good German and Spanish. He grew up in Boston so his English has that New England 'twang' to it."

"That's good to know, Igor. But you haven't told us your whole name. Igor is fine, but there's more, isn't there?"

"Sure. It's Igor Mikhailovich Popov, Popov being one of the most common names in all of Russia."

Traffic on the way to the embassy was slow and messy, stop and go for many kilometers. When Igor finally arrived at the embassy's rear entrance, his two passengers were exhausted.

"Thanks for the ride, Igor, the next time we need a driver, you'll be the one we'll call. C'mon, Natasha, let's find our apartment, call it a day, and go to bed."

Three

0830 THE NEXT MORNING. OXNER HAS finished shaving and finds that his wife is already up and dressed.

"They say the early bird gets the worm. How long have you been up?"

"Robert, you won't believe what I found, just a few minutes ago."

"So, tell me."

"First, there's a large bouquet of red roses with a note attached, written by ambassador Jenkins. It says 'Welcome to your new assignment, we'll talk later.' Then in the fridge there's two cartons of whole milk, a dozen eggs, marmalade, strawberry jam, a package of that pre-cooked bacon, a head of lettuce, small jars of mayo and mustard, a small piece of Russian sausage, and in the freezer a small bottle of Stolichnaya vodka, which we can do without."

"Beer?"

"Yes. A six-pack of Heinekens, imported from Denmark."

"Okay, Sweetheart. Our appointment with the ambassador is just fifteen minutes away, so let's get dressed, say a prayer, and go!"

"No, wait, Robert. There's something we need to do first."

"What's that, Natasha?"

"It's something I just learned, after searching my laptop. I, we, should have thought about this before. Apparently there's at least one clinic here in Moscow that treats mothers and their infant children who have become drug addicts, usually heroin but a synthetic drug that the young people know as speed. It's awful stuff, Robert, and according to what I just read this particular clinic can't accept any more patients; they're asking the Moscow authorities for permission to open at least three more and that's because the doctor at one of these clinics has learned that many of the patients are wives and children of ranking members of president Putin's staff. So you can see the potential here; those few Russians who dare oppose the president can begin to tell others about this no-longer-secret."

At last, in ambassador Jenkin's office

"Finally, we meet. Your predecessor told me that you'd be able to step right in where he left off, so the transition should be smooth enough."

"Thanks for that, Mr. Ambassador. But before we talk shop, my wife has something to say. Go ahead, Natasha."

"Yes. We can't thank you enough for the way our apartment is arranged and the things we found in the kitchen. Small things, yes, but they make it easier for the two of us to become adjusted to living here in Moscow."

"Robert, I'm curious to know how you see yourself as the CIA's new Chief of Station. Everyone in this building already knows who you are and what your cover situation is all about. How do you feel about this?"

"Shouldn't be a problem, Sir. I've served with most of these people at other posts, we know each other, each of them speaks Russian, so I don't see anything to worry about.

"And before we go back to our apartment I'd like to know what you consider to be our most important challenge, in terms of America's security."

"It's an easy question but the answer is likely to be difficult. I'm talking about what's happening down south in our Caucasus region. As you certainly must know, Chechnya and Dagestan are still trying to persuade the Kremlin to allow them to secede and establish their own country. After you've had time to get settled, you should come back to your office and read about it. It's a piece that was written by one of my staff."

Four hours later, Oxner is seated at his desk and begins to read.

Deep in the rolling hills of Southwest Russia's mountainous Caucasus region lies a pair of restive territories, home to a once nomadic collection of ethnic groups. The Avars and the Chechens, who call the north Caucasus region their home, represent a modern distinct identity whose struggle for independence is decades old. The Chechen's history was especially marred following the collapse of the USSR, after which the Russian Federation executed a ruthless campaign to silence the unremitting cause for Chechen independence. With their ancient roots too closely tied and similar to those of other ethnic communities around the world, the people of Dagestan and Chechnya represent a new type of conflict that may reshape the geopolitical and cultural landscape of the modern world.

After a chain of migrations of various ethnic populations in ancient times from locations such as the Fertile Crescent as well as Northeast and Central Asia, what came to be known as the Chechen and Avar peoples settled in the Northern Caucasus region. For centuries this was the site of various invasions and imperial conflicts, involving empires such as the Cimmerians, Mongols, Scythians, Persians, Ottomans, and Safavids.

It was not until 1859 at the end of the Caucasian War that the Chechens and Avars would meet their greatest challenge, which still torments them today. At the dawn of the 19th century, Russian Tsar Nicholas I commanded a years-long invasion of the Caucasus region. The Circassian Genocide became the first of many forced exiles of Chechens by Russian Imperial Forces. By the conclusion of the Russo-Persian wars, this entire region fell under the control of Imperial Russia, an event which would define the rebellion of the native people thereafter.

A century and a half later, in what was then known as the Chechen-Ingush Autonomous Soviet Socialist Republic, one of the first serious Chechen rebellions ignited. The rebellion began in 1940 under Chechen leader Khasan Israilov and was impassioned by the German invasion of the Caucasus in 1942. However, the first Chechen insurgency was killed off in 1944 after the Germans scaled back their presence and when rebels began defecting to the Soviet Union. In response to this, Joseph Stalin deported Chechens in massive numbers from the Caucasus, scattering them across the territories of the USSR, some as far as Kazakhstan and Kyrgyzstan.

Decades after the fury of the Second World War died out, a new flame was struck ablaze in 1944 within the Caucasus mountains. The people of Chechnya desired independence from their Russian overlords.

Although the First Chechen War lasted only two years, the scars it left on the Caucasus region would not be forgotten. The devastating Battle of Grozny in 1996 saw Chechen forces holding out against the advancements of Russian artillery into the mountainous regions. The Chechens employed guerilla warfare and attacks on the flatlands for sufficiently long enough that Russian President Boris Yeltsin declared a cease fire in August 1996. Shortly after, a new conflict broke out that would directly include the territory of Dagestan.

In the fall of 1999, Islamist forces from Chechnya infiltrated Dagestan and declared a Jihadist separatist movement to cleanse the region of "unbelievers." Meanwhile, in Chechnya, Russian troops entered the restored Russia's Federal rule over the entire region. For the following nine years, heavy military offensives ravaged the Chechnyan capital of Grozny, while Chechen paramilitary separatists engaged in violent combat with Russian counter-insurgency troops. By 2009, the Chechen rebellion was largely crippled, with only marginal resistance scattered throughout the Northern Caucasus.

THE SITUATION TODAY

The relative silence in the wake of the fallen Chechen revolution created a fertile breeding ground for latent animosity, which harms both Russia's mainland and the Chechens themselves. In cases where ethnic minorities advocate a cause for independence from a greater geo-political force, radicalism in their ranks is the downfall of their claims to legitimacy. For instance, the East Turkestan Independence Movement is often used to defame the words of peaceful Uyghur human rights activists. This is because ETIM has been linked to external extremist Islamist movements and a very small portion of Uyghur individuals traveled to Syria to fight with the Islamic State. By the same token, within Chechnya and Dagestan, jihadist cells lie dormant before committing atrocities and acts of terror in the Russian mainland to convey their messages—unfortunately destroying the image of their Muslim brothers in the Caucasus.

One of the most turbulent events occurred when more than forty terrorists took hostage nearly 700 patrons of a theater in Moscow. The captors demanded that the Russian government surrender its control over Chechnya and end its presence in the region. Ultimately, Russian Federal Security Service spetsnaz operators pumped a highly toxic gas into the theater before attempting their rescue operation, ultimately killing hundreds of civilians in the process to subdue the attackers.

This, among other mutually destructive confrontations between Russian and militant Chechens, in the aftermath of the second war, bore a much deeper hole in their tumultuous relationship. Unfortunately, the small portion of Chechens who take up arms against the Russians make the case of Chechnyan independence much more strained. The massive casualties on either side paint a misleading picture of hatred and radicalism, two images which chill the international community.

Dagestan, Chechnya's geopolitical sister, presents a different story today. The regions share many similarities, such as their history and desire for autonomy, but many factors of modern-day Dagestan's composition make it a very different environment from Chechnya. Dagestan's population is diverse, with nearly 30 different spoken languages and ten different ethnic groups, compared with Chechnya's population of more than 95% Chechens. A combination of secrecy and demographic heterogeneity make Dagestan's war seemingly less explosive, when in reality, it is, if not equally, nearly as catastrophic as Chechnya's war with Russia.

For the most part, Dagestani authorities attempted to prevent the same level of turbulence in Chechnya, but violent spillover during the Chechen wars scarred Dagestan's territories as well. Radical Islamism is also a grave issue growing in the troubled minds of Dagestan's younger population. Younger Muslims in Dagestan are turning more from Sufi towards Salafi Islam, which is generously adherent to more puritanical and concrete principles—a perfect channel through which Dagestanis may funnel their political vitriol into campaigns of hatred against the Russians.

Islamism would heavily oversimplify the plight of the Dagestanis though; they too face the weight of Russia's government corruption and human rights abuses. Russian President Vladimir Putin, in his continued efforts to enforce a zero-tolerance policy on violence in Dagestan, began sending military generals to command brutal campaigns against any resistance within the restive Islamic region. Dagestan's history and similarity to Chechnya taunt Putin, as it seems any other uprising in the Caucasus would trigger much more violence and unavoidable scrutiny against the Kremlin. For now, Russia maintains its operations in Dagestan as secretive as possible while the region receives fleeting media attention, but this approach fools nobody. Dagestan is not the same as Chechnya, but their stories resonate ominously with one another—a constant reminder that Dagestan, too, is on the verge of surges in violence and a devastating retaliation from the Kremlin.

Low level violence and skirmishes continue through-out Chechnya, with active protests ringing throughout the streets of Grozny. The tensons affect outsiders as well, with supporters of Chechen rights being targeted by Russian loyalists as traitors. Russia is a global power with stakes in multiple conflicts, and its relationship with its minority territories sets a dangerous precedent for nations like it. Sinister human rights abuses are occurring worldwide in the small pockets of much larger nations, and the people, if not overshadowed, are easily castigated as villainous when onlookers attribute the most radical of them as tributes to the whole. Amidst a changing world, the people of Dagestan and Chechnya will only make progress towards independence if each one of them lays down arms against Russia. But with such hostile attitudes towards their ethnicity and an already-vicious campaign to silence the greater Russian LGBTQ+ community, the starkly lacking human rights make hostile encroachment nearly inevitable.

Dagestan and Chechnya are not alone in their fight against one of the world's largest superpowers. Their fight is echoed strongly by their Islamic brethren to the east: the Uyghurs inhabiting Xinjiang province in China. The Uyghur are not only of similar Altaic and Turkic descent, but their people's history is colored with conquest beneath Indo-European and Sino-Tibetan Empires through which their culture and identity persevered; that is, until their confrontation with the Qing Dynasty in the 18th century. Now, the Chinese Communist Party brutally scrutinizes their inhabitation of the Tarm Basin, via extremely invasive modes of surveillance and control. The same can be said of the Rohingya people's accusation of Rakhine State in Western Myanmar, which was met with militaristic genocide at the hands of the Burmese government in August 2017, or of the Kurdish inhabitants of Northeast Syria, Iraq and Turkey where the

Kurds reputedly face the existential threats of terrorism and invasions.

Millions upon millions of people around the world, whose radiant cultures give shape to their unique identities, live in oppressed communities where their geography remains governed by immense federations whose power bases overshadow their cries for freedom. The international community, however, is becoming increasingly aware of these conflicts, but this may be as much of a disadvantage as it is a marker of hope.

In a post-9/11 world, global mindsets have a much lower threshold for extremist activity. When people actually hear of real-life extremism, their attitudes towards conflicts shift drastically in favor of those trying to contain the purported terrorism. While the world hears about Dagestan, the Chechens, the Uyghurs, the Rohingya and more, there is a sharp dichotomy between advocating for human rights and scapegoating draconian measures to contain the faintest chances of terrorist activity by any means. Sadly, Chechnya's prolific violence sways the picture towards the side of terrorism. Russia's global confrontations may not come to a head anytime soon, but the world is changing and many eyes are fixating on the Eurasian superpower in time where regional conflicts are bringing out the worst in governments. Chechnya's future is defined by the Chechen people's collective willpower to defer violent measures in resisting Russian control.

"Hmm, whoever wrote this certainly knew what he was talking about. And he's right, of course. Chechnya and Dagestan can continue to push the Russian leadership, to insist that they have the right to secede and establish their own nation. But what, if anything, can the United States do to help? Or the better question is should we try to help? As one, independent nation, whose leadership is Islamic, it would have control of the entire Caspian Sea, from Astrakhan in the north, to any number of Persian ports to the south. And Iran has been a sworn enemy of the United States ever since the 1979 hostage crisis. No, best we stay out of this. There are more important things to worry about."

Four

1 000 HOURS, IN AMBASSADOR JENKIN'S OFFICE. Oxner and his wife are about to recommend a plan.

"Mr. Ambassador, Natasha and I have talked about this but it's something you should know."

"Yes. But before we get to that I have something here that just came across my desk, a total surprise. It's an e-mail from Roman Arkadyevich Abramovich, one of these so-called Russian oligarchs. What's amazing about this is what he's telling us. He says he has a brother who is working in New York City as a financial advisor. The brother has been there for three years and says he knows that that Americans are a live-and-let-live people. And he wants his brother Roman to consider joining him. Of course that would be a dangerous thing to do if it's not planned properly.

And he's provided a kind of personal history statement to prove that he is who he says he is.

ROMAN ARKADYEVICH ABROMOVICH, BORN OCTOBER 24, 1966 in Saratov, USSR, is Russian businessman and politician. He is the former of Chelsea, a Premier League football club in London, and is the primary owner of the private investment company Millhouse. He has Russian, Israeli and Portuguese citizenship.

He was formerly governor of Chukotka Autonomous Okrug from 2000 to 2008. According to Forbes his net worth was US$14.5 billion in 2021, making him the second-richest person in Israel. Since then, his wealth decreased to $6.9 billion and recovered up to $9.2 billion in 2023. He enriched himself in the years following the collapse of the Soviet Union in the 1990s, obtaining Russian state-owned assets at prices far below market value in Russia's controversial loans-for-shares privatization program. He is considered to have a good relationship with Russian president Vladimir Putin, an allegation Abramovich has denied.

His mother, Irena, was a music teacher who died when Abramovich was one year old. His father, Aaron Abramovich Leibovich, who was of Jewish descent, worked in the economic council of the Komi ASSR, and died when Roman was three. Roman's maternal grandparents were Vasily Mikhailenko and Faina Borisovna Grutman, both born in Ukraine. It was to Saratov in the early days of World War II that Roman's maternal grandmother fled from Ukraine. Irina was three years old. Roman's paternal grandparents, Nachman Leibovich and Tatayana Stepanovona Abramovich, were Belarusian Jews. They lived in Belarus and, after the revolution, moved to Taurge, Lithuania, with the Lithuanian spelling of the family name being Abramavicius.

IN 1940, THE SOVIET UNION ANNEXED Lithuania. Just before the Nazi German invasion of the USSR, the Soviets "cleared the anti-Soviet, criminal and socially dangerous element" with whole families being sent to Siberia.

Abramovich's grandparents were separated and deported. The father, mother, and children—Leib, Abram, and Aron—were in different camps. Many of the deportees died in the camps.

Among them was the grandfather of Abramovich. Nachman Leibovich died in 1942 in the NKVD camp in the settlement of Resheti, Krasnoyarsk Territory.

Having lost both parents before the age of four, Abramovich was raised by relatives and spent much of his youth in the Komi Republic in northern Russia.

HE IS THE CHAIRMAN OF THE Federation of Jewish Communities of Russia, and a trustee of the Moscow Museum. Abramovich decided to establish a forest of some 25,000 new and rehabilitated trees, in memory of Lithuania's Jews who were murdered in the Holocaust, plus a virtual memorial and tribute to Lithuanian Jewry, enabling people from all over the world to commemorate their ancestors' personal stories by naming a tree and including their name in the memorial.

ABROMOVICH ENTERED THE BUSINESS WORLD DURING his army service. He first worked as a street trader and then as mechanic at a local factory. He attended the Gubkin Institute of Oil and Gas in Moscow, then traded commodities for the Swiss trading firm Runicom.

In 1998, as perestroika created opportunities for privatization in the Soviet Union, Abramovich gained a chance to legitimize his old business. He and his first wife, Olga, set up a company making dolls. Within a few years his wealth spread from oil conglomerates to pig farms. He has traded in timber, sugar, foodstuffs, and other products.

In 1992 he was arrested and sent to prison in a case of theft of government property.

ACCORDING TO TWO DIFFERENT SOURCES, ABRAMOVICH first met Berezovsky either at a meeting with the Russian businessmen in 1993 or in the summer of 1995. The two men registered an offshore company, Runicom Ltd, with five subsidiaries. Abromovich headed the Moscow affiliate of the Swiss firm, Runicom. In August 1995, Boris Yeltsin decreed the creation of Sibneft, of which Abramovich and Berezovsky were though to be top executives.

In 1995, Abramovich and Berezovsky acquired a controlling interest in the large oil company Sibneft in a rigged election. The deal took place within the controversial loans for shares program and each partner paid US$150 million at the time and rapidly turned it up into billions. The fast-rising value of the company led many observers, in hindsight, to suggest that the real cost of the company should have been in the billions of dollars. Abramovich later admitted in court that he paid billions of dollars in bribes to government officials and gangsters to protect his assets. As of 2000, Sibneft annually produced $US 3 billion worth of oil.

The Times (Moscow) claimed that he was assisted by Badri Lomidze in the acquisition of Sibneft. After Sibneft, Abramovich's next target was the aluminum industry. After privatization the "aluminum wars" led to murders of smelting plant managers, metals traders and journalists as groups battled for control of the industry. Abramovich was initially hesitant to enter into the aluminum business, claiming that "every three days someone was murdered in that business." Abramovich sold Sibneft to the Russian government for $13 billion in 2005.

In 2011, Abramovich's longtime business partner filed a suit, Berezovsky v. Abramovich in the High Court of Justice in London. He accused Abramovich of blackmail, breach of trust, and breach of contract. The suit sought more than 3 billion British pounds in damages.

On August 31, 2012, the High Court dismissed the lawsuit. The judge stated that because of the nature of the evidence, the case hinged on whether to believe Berezovsky or Abramovich's evidence. The judge found Berezovsky to be "an unimpressive and inherently unreliable witness" who regarded truth as a transitory, flexible concept, which could be moulded to suit his current purposes, whereas Abramovich was seen as a "truthful and on the whole, reliable witness."

In 2011, a transcript emerged of a taped conversation that took place between Abramovich and Berezovsky at Le Bourget airport in December 2000. Badri Lomidze, a close acquaintance of Berezovsky, was also present and secretly had the conversation recorded.

During the discussion, Berezovsky spoke of how they should "legalize" their aluminum business and later claim in court that he was an undisclosed shareholder in the aluminum assets and that "legalization" in this case meant to make his ownership "official." In response, Abramovich states in the transcript that they cannot legalize because the other party in the 50 – 50 venture (Rusal) would need to do the same, in a supposed reference to his business partner Oleg Deripaska. Besides Deripaska, references are made to several other players in the aluminum industry at the time that would have had to legalize their stake. Abramovich's lawyers later claimed that "legalization" meant structuring protection payments to Berezovsky to ensure they complied with Western antimony-laundering regulations.

The Times also observed that there was a showdown at the St Moritz airport in Switzerland in 2001 when Mr. Lomidze asked him to pay US$1.3 billion to Mr. Berezovsky. "The defendant agreed to pay this amount on the basis that it would be final request for payment by Mr. Berezovsky and that he and Mr. Lomidze would cease to associate themselves publicly with him and his business interests." The payment was duly made.

Mr. Abramovich was also willing to pay off Mr. Lomidze. He states that he agreed to pay US$585 million "by way of a final payment."

Mr. Abramovich denies that he helped himself to Mr. Berezovsky's interests in Sibneft and aluminum or that he threatened a friend of the exile. "It is denied that Mr. Abramovich made or was party to the alleged explicit or implicit coercive threats or intimidation," he states.

According to court papers submitted by Abramovich, he writes:

> Prior to the August 1995 decree of Sibneft's creation, the defendant informed Mr. Berezovsky that he wished to acquire a controlling interest in Sibneft on its creation. In return for the defendant agreeing to provide Mr. Berezovsky with funds he required in connection with the cash flow of his TV company ORT, Mr. Berezovsky agreed he would use his personal and political influence to support the project and assist in the passage of the necessary legislative steps leading to the creation of Sibneft. R. Lomidze did provide assistance to the defendant in the defendant's acquisition of assets in the Russian aluminum industry.

In 2005, Abramovich invested and led a $30 million round of funding with businessman O.D. Kobo, Chairman of PIR Equities. Other partners include several well-known people from the music industry, among them David Guetta, Nicki Minaj, Benny Andersson, David Holmes, and others.

Also StoreDot, founded by Doron Myersdorf, where Abramovich has invested more that $30 million.

In June 2003, Abromovich became the owner of the companies that control Chelsea, in West London. The previous owner of the club was Ken Bates, who later bought rivals Leeds United. Chelsea immediately embarked on an ambitious program of commercial development, with the aim of making it a world wide brand at par with football dynasties such as Manchester United and Real Madrid, and also announced plans to build a new state-of-the-art training complex in Cobham, Surrey.

Since the takeover, the club has won 18 major trophies—the UEFA Champions League twice, the UEFA Europa League twice, the UEFA Supercup twice, the Premier League five times, and the FA Cup five times, making Chelsea the most successful English trophy winning team during Abramovich's ownership, equal with Manchester United. His tenure has also been marked by rapid turnover in managers. Detractors have used the term "Chelski" to refer to the new Chelsea under Abramovich, to highlight the modern phenomena of billionaires buying football clubs and "purchasing trophies" by using their personal wealth to snap up marquee players at will and distorting the transfer market, citing the acquisition of Andriy Shevchenko for a then-British record transfer fee of about 30 million British pounds.

In the year ending June 2005, Chelsea posted record losses of 140 million pounds and the club was not expected to record a trading profit before 2010, although this decreased to reported losses of 80.2 million pounds in the year ending June 2006. In a December 2006 interview, Abramovich stated that he expected Chelsea's transfer spending to fall in the years to come. UEFA responded to the precarious profit/loss landscape of clubs, some owned by billionaires but others simply financial juggernauts like Real Madrid, with Financial Fair Ply regulations. Chelsea finished their first season after the takeover in second place in the Premier League, up from fourth the previous year. They also reached the semi-finals for the Champions League, which was eventually won by the surprise contender Porto, managed by Jose Mourinho. For Abramovich's second season at Stamford Bridge, Mourinho was recruited as the new manager, replacing the incumbent Claudio Ranieri. Chelsea ended the 2004-05 season as league champions, for the first time in 50 years and only the second time in their history. Also high were Abramovich's spending regarding purchases of Portuguese football players. According to record newspaper accounts, he spent 165.1 Euros in Portugal: 90.9 with Benfica players and 74.2 with Porto players.

During his stewardship of the club, Abramovich was present at nearly every Chelsea game and showed visible emotion during matches, a sign taken by supporters to indicate a genuine love for the sport, and often visited the players in the dressing room following each match. This stopped for a time in early 2007, when press reports appeared of a feud between Abromovich and manager Mourinho regarding the performance of certain players such as Andrey Shevchenko.

On July 1, 2013, Chelsea celebrated ten years under Abramovich's ownership. Before the first game of the 2013-2014 season against Hull City on August 18, 2013, Abramovich thanked Chelsea supporters for ten years of support, in a short message on the front cover of the match program, saying, "We have had a great decade together and the club could not have achieved it all without you. Thanks for your support and here's to many more years of success."

In March 2017, Chelea announced it had received approval for a revamped 500 million pound stadium at Stamford Bridge with a capacity of up to 60,000.

On July 15, 2018, with the renewal of Abramovich's British visa by the Home Office, and his subsequent withdrawal of the application, in May 2018, Chelsea halted plans to build a 500 million pound stadium in southwest London, due to the "unfavorable investment climate" and the lack of assurances about Abramovich's immigration status. Abramovich was set to invest hundreds of millions of pounds for the construction of the stadium. He has been accused of purchasing Chelsea at the behest of Vladimir Putin, but he has denied the claim.

Putin's People, a book by journalist Catherin Belton, a former

Financial Times Moscow correspondent, formerly made such an assertion, but after libel action by Abramovich against Belton and the book's publisher Harper Collins, the claims were agreed in December 2021 to be stated as having no factual basis in future editions.

In 2021, Abramovich was criticized for trying to enter Chelse into the newly announced European Super League. The competition was widely scrutinized for encouraging greediness among the richer, larger football clubs, which would have undermined the significance of existing football competitions; however, just two days later, Abramovich pulled the club out of the new competition, with other English cubs following suit, causing the league to suspend operations. In 2022, it was reported that Abramovich was owed $2 billion from Chelsea.

According to *Forbes*, Abramovich's loan was insurance in case the British government considered sanctioning him due to his close relationship with the Putin regime in Russia.

On February 26, 2022, during the Russo-Ukrainian War, Abramovich handed over "stewardship and care" of the club to the Chelsea Charitable Foundation.

Abramovich released an official statement on March 2, 2022, confirming that he was selling the club due to the ongoing situation in Ukraine. Although the UK government froze Abramovich's assets in the United Kingdom on March 10, due to his "close ties with the Kremlin," it was made clear that the Chelsea club would be allowed to operate in activities which were football-related.

On March 12, the Premier League disqualified Abramovich as a director of Chelsea.

On May 7, 2022, Chelsea announced that a new ownership group led by Todd Boehy and Clearlake Capital had agreed on the terms to acquire the club.

In March 2004, Sibneft agreed to a three-year sponsorship deal worth $58 million with the Russian team CSKA Moscow. Although the company explained that the decision was made at management level, some viewed the deal as an attempt by Abramovich to counter accusations of being "unpatriotic" which were made at the time of the Celsea purchase. UEFA rules prevent one person owning more than one team participating in UEFA competitions, so Abramovich has no equity interest in CSKA. A lawyer, Alexander Garese, is one his partners in CSKA.

Following an investigation, Abramovich was cleared by UEFA of having a conflict of interest. Nevertheless, he was named "most influential person in Russian football" in the Russian magazine *Pro Sport* at the end of June 2004.

In May 2005, CSKA won the UEFA Cup, becoming the first Russian club ever to win a major European football competition. In October 2005, however, Abramovich sold his interest in Sibneft and the company's new owner Gazprom, which sponsors Zenit St. Petersburg, cancelled the sponsorship deal.

Abramovich also played a large role in bringing Guus Hiddink to Russia to coach the Russia national football team. Piet de Visser, a former head scout of Hiddink's club PSV Eindhoven and now a personal assistant to Abramovich at Chelsea, recommended Hiddink to the Chelsea owner.

In addition to his involvement in professional football, Abramovich sponsors a foundation in Russia called the National Academy of Football. The organization sponsors youth sports programs throughout the country and has constructed more than fifty football pitches in various cities and towns, prints instructional materials, renovates sports facilities and takes top coaches and students on trips to visit professional football club in England, the Netherlands, and Spain. In 2006 the Academy of Football took over the administration of the Konoplyov football academy at Primorsky, near Togliatti, Samara Oblast, where more than 1,000 youths are in residence, following the death at 38 of its founder, Yuri Konoplev.

A statement from Abramovich:

"Everyone's got their own reasons. Some believe it's because I spent some of my childhood in the far north, that I helped Chukotka, some believe it's because I had a difficult childhood, that I helped Chukotka, some believe it's because I stole money that I helped Chukotka. None of these is real. When you come out and you see a situation and there are 50,000 people, you want to do something. I haven't seen anything worse than what I saw there in my life."

IN 1999, ABRAMOVICH WAS ELECTED TO the State Duma as the representative for the Chukotka Autonomous Okrug, an impoverished region in the Russian Far East. He started the charity Pole of Hope to help the people of Chukotka, especially children, and in December 2000, was elected governor of Chukotka, replacing Aleksandr Nazarov.

Abramovich was the governor of Chukotka from 2000 to 2008. It is believed that he invested more than $1.3 billion in the region. He was awarded the Order of Honor for his "huge contribution to the economic development of the autonomous district of Chukotka," by a decree signed by the President of Russia.

In early July 2008, it was announced that President Dmitry Medvedev had accepted Abramovich's request to resign as governor of Chukotka, although his various charitable activities in the region would continue. In the period 2000-2006, the average salaries in Chukotka increased from about US$165 per month to US$826 per month.

THE DAY AFTER THE 2022 RUSSIAN invasion of Ukraine, Abramovich was contacted by Ukrainian magnates and asked to function as an informal envoy to Putin.

He played a key role in the release of Aiden Aslin and other foreign prisoners of war from Russian captivity.

ABRAMOVICH IS ONE OF MANY RUSSIAN oligarchs named in the Countering America's Adversaries Through Sanctions Act, signed into law by president Donald Trump in 2017.

Following the Russian invasion of Ukraine in 2022, on March 10 Abramovich was sanctioned by the UK as part of a group of seven Russian oligarchs. Abramovich had his UK assets frozen and a travel ban was put in place. The British government said the sanctions were in response to Abramovich's alleged ties to the Kremlin and said the companies Abramovich controls could be producing steel used in tanks deployed offensively by Russia in Ukraine. Abramovich denies that he has close ties to Vladimir Putin and the Kremlin.

Also on March 10, Canada imposed sanctions against Abramovich as a businessman helping Vladimir Putin in his war against Ukraine. On March 14, Australia and on March 15, the European Union followed Britain's suit and also imposed sanctions on Abramovich.

On March 16, Abramovich was added to the Swiss blacklist. On April 5 2022, Abramovich came under New Zealand sections for close ties with Vladimir Putin.

On October 19, Volodymyr Zelensky signed two decrees imposing personal sanctions against 256 Russian businessmen. Among these was Abramovich, being the only person on the list, the restrictions against whom will only work after the exchange of all Ukrainian prisoners and bodies of those killed during the Russian invasion of Ukraine.

In late March 2022, it was reported that Abramovich was house-hunting in Dubai, where his private plane had also been spotted, owing to the city's sanction-free status.

In March 2022, *The Wall Street Journal* reported that the United States administration deferred sanctions on Abramovich at the urging of President of Ukraine Volodymyr Zelensky, because of the oligarch's potential role in negotiations with Russia. The Russian government spokesperson Dmitry Peskov confirmed that Abramovich took part in the negotiations "at the initial stage." No further details of the nature of Abramovich's involvement in the process were disclosed by either party to the conflict.

In December 2022, Canada announced that it would target him for the maiden use of its SEMA seizure and forfeiture mechanism. The government alleged that US$26 million held by Granite Capital Holdings Ltd was in fact Abramovich's and stated that it 'will now consider making a court application to forfeit the Abramovich assets permanently to the Crown.

In December 2023, Abramovich failed to overturn the EU sanctions, when the Court of Justice of the European Union dismissed his lawsuit.

On March 3 and 4, 2022, Abromovich attended peace talks on the Ukraine-Belarus border. Abramovich, Ukrainian politician Rustem Umierov, and one other negotiator suffered initial symptoms consistent with likely poisoning with an unknown chemical substance, involving "piercing pain in the eyes," inflammation of the eyes and skin with some skin peeling. They all recovered quickly. Bellingcat investigated the allegation and said that chocolate or water that the three had consumed may have been laced with poison; experts took samples of the substance but were unable to identify the type of material used, owing to the passage of time. Western sources said the low dosage of poison was aimed to serve as a warning, most likely to Abramovich, and suspected the attack may have been carried ou by hardliners in Moscow who tried to sabotage peace talks. An unnamed U.S. official said that the illness was caused by "environmental factors" rather than poisoning. Additionally, an official in the Ukrainian president's office, Igor Zhovkva informed the BBC that while he hadn't spoken to Mr. Abramovich, participants of the Ukrainian delegation were "fine" and one had said the story was "false." Frank Gardiner of the BBC said the U.S. denial may be caused by a reluctance to respond in a retaliatory manner to Russia by accepting the deployment of chemical weapons in Ukraine. A spokesman for Ukrainian president Volodymyr Zelensky said that he had no information about a suspected poisoning.

BY 1996, AT THE AGE OF 30, Abramovich had become close to President Boris Yeltsin an had moved into an apartment inside the Kremlin, at the invitation of the Yeltsin family.

In 1999, the 33-year-old Abramovich was elected governor of the Russian province of Chukotka. He ran for a second term as governor in 2005. The Kremlin press service reported that Abramovich's name had been sent for approval s governor for another term to Chukotka's local parliament, which confirmed his appointment on October 21, 2005.

ABRAMOVICH WAS THE FIRST PERSON TO recommend to Yeltsin that Vladimir Putin be his successor as the Russian president. When Putin formed his first cabinet as Prim Minister in 1999, Abramovich interviewed each of the candidates for cabinet positions before they were approved. Subsequently, Abramovich would remain one of Putin's closest confidants. In 2007, Putin consulted in meetings with Abramovich on the question of who should be his successor's president; Medvedev was personally recommended by Abramovich.

CHRIS HUTCHINS, A BIOGRAPHER OF PUTIN, described the relationship between the Russian president and Abramovich as like that between a father and a favorite son. In the early 2000s,

Abramovich said that when he addressed Putin he uses the Russian language's formal "You" as a mark of respect for Putin's seniority. Within the Kremlin, Abramovich was referred to as "Mr. A."

IN SEPTEMBER 2012, THE ENGLAND AND Wales High Court judge Elizabeth Gloster claimed that Abramovich's influence on Putin was limited. "There was no evidential basis supporting the contention that Mr. Abramovich was in a position to manipulate, or otherwise influence, President Putin, or officers in his administration, to exercise their powers in such a way as to enable Mr. Abramovich to achieve his own commercial goals."

Gloster oversaw the case between Russian oligarchs Boris Berezovsky and Abramovich. She found Berezovsky to be "an inherently unreliable witness" and sided with Abramovich in 2012. It later emerged that Gloster's stepson had been paid almost a half-million British pounds to represent Abramovich as a barrister early in the case. Her stepson's involvement was alleged to be more than had been disclosed. Berezovsky stated, "Sometimes I have the impression that Putin himself wrote this judgment." Gloster declined to comment.

IN 2021, IT WAS REPORTED BY *The Washington Examiner* that the U.S. intelligence community believes Abramovich is a "bag carrier," or a financial middleman, for Putin.

IN 2011, BORIS BEREZOVSKY BROUGHT A civil case against Abramovich, called Berezovsky v. Abramovich, in the High Court of Justice in London, but Berezovsky was unsuccessful in the case.

In 2008 *The Times* reported that court papers showed Abramovich admitting that he paid billions of dollars for political favors and protection fees for shares in Russia's oil and aluminum assets.

AN ALLEGATION EMERGING FROM A SWISS investigation links Roman Abramovich, through a former company, and numerous other Russian politicians, industrialists, and bankers to using a US$4.8 billion loan from the IMF as a personal slush fund; an audit sponsored by the IMF itself determined that all of the IMF funds had been used appropriately.

IN JANUARY 2005, THE EUROPEAN BANK for Reconstruction and Development indicated that it would be suing Abramovich over a US$14.9 million loan. The EBRD said that it is owed US$17.5 million by Runicom, a Switzerland-based oil trading business which had been controlled by Abromovich and Eugene Shvidler. Abramovich's spokesman indicated that the loan had previously been repaid.

Russia's antitrust body, the Federal Antimonopoly Service, claimed that Evraz Holding, owned in part by Abramovich, had breached Russian competition law by offering unfavorable terms for contractors and discriminating against domestic consumers for coking coal, a key material used in steel production.

ACCORDING TO PUTIN, ABRAMOVICH HAS BEEN cheated by Ukrainian-Cypriot-Israeli oligarch Igor Kolomoysky. Putin claimed in 2014 that the man had reneged on a contract with Abromovich, saying that the pair signed a multibillion deal on which the man never delivered.

According to *The Guardian*, in 2015 his $766 million stake in Evraz, the steel and mining company, gave him ownership of about a quarter of Russia's largest coal mine, the Raspadskaya coal complex in Siberia, whose reserves represented 1.5 tons of carbon emissions, comparable to the annual output of Russia itself.

ACCORDING TO THE CONVERSATION, "ROMAN ABRAMOVICH, who made most of his $19 billion fortune trading in gas and oil, was the biggest polluter on our list of most polluting billionaires," estimating that "he was responsible for at least 33, 859 tons of CO_2 emissions in 2018—more than two-thirds from his yacht."

AN INVESTIGATION BY BBC NEWS ARABIC has found that Abramovich controls companies that have donated $100 million to an Israeli settler organization, Elad, which aims to strengthen the Jewish connection to the annexed East Jerusalem, and renew the Jewish community in the City of David. Analysis of bank documents indicate Abramovich is the largest single donor to the organization. The bank documents, known as the FinCen Files were leaked to BuzzFeed News, then shared with the International consortium of Investigative Journalists and the BBC.

ABRAMOVICH IS DESCRIBED BY THOSE CLOSE to him as naturally secretive, reserved, calculating, efficient, and devoid of feeling and values. He often dresses simply. He is described as shy and rarely makes eye contact. *Le Monde* claimed his personal character contrasts with that of other oligarchs.

He has been married and divorced three times. In December 1987, following a brief stint in the Soviet Army, he married a former Russian Aeroflot stewardess, Irina Malandina. They have five children: Illya, Arnina, Sofia, Arkadiy, and Anna. His eldest daughter Anna is a graduate of Columbia University and lives in New York City, His daughter Sofia is a professional equestrian who lives in London, after graduating from Royal Holloway, University of London.

On October 15, 2006, the *News of the World* reported that Irina had hired two top UK divorce lawyers, following reports of Abramovich's close relationship with the then 25-year-old Dasha Zhukova, daughter of a prominent Russian oligarch, Alexander

Zhukov. The Abramoviches replied that neither had consulted attorneys at that point. However, they later divorced in Russia in March 2007, with a reported settlement of US$300 million.

Abramovich married Zhukova in 2008 and they have two children, a son Aaron Alexander, and a daughter Leah Lou. In August 2017, the couple announced that they would separate and their divorce was finalized in 2018.

In May 2018, Abramovich became an Israeli citizen a month after the UK delayed renewing his visa. Following the poisoning of Sergei and Yulia Skripal, British authorities delayed the renewal of his visa, as tensions rose between the UK and Russia. Abramovich had been travelling in and out of the UK for years on a Tier-1 investor visa, designed for wealthy foreigners who invest at least two million pounds in Britain.

ABRAMOVICH, WHO IS RUSSIAN-JEWISH, EXERCISED HIS birthright under Israel's Law of Return, which states that Jews from anywhere in the world can become citizens of Israel. As an Israeli, Abramovich can now visit Britain visa-free but is not permitted to work or conduct business transactions.

ABRAMOVICH OWNS THE VARSANO BOUTIQUE HOTEL in the Neve Tedek neighborhood of Tel Aviv, Israel, which he bought for 100 million English pounds, this in 2015 from Israeli actress and model Gal Gadot's husband Yaron Varsano and his brother Guy. In January 2020, Abramovich purchased a property in Herzliiya Pituah, Israel for a record 226 million English pounds.

In 2015, Abramovich donated approximately $30 million to Tel Aviv University to establish an innovative center for nanoscience and nanotechnology, which aspires to become one of the leading facilities in the Middle East. Among his other beneficiaries is the Sheba Medical Center in Tel HaShomer, Israel, to which he has donated in excess of $60 million for various advanced medicine ventures. These include the establishment of a new nuclear medicine center spanning 2,000 square meters, the Sheba Cancer and Cancer Research Centers, the Pediatric Middle East Congenital Heart Center, and the Sheba Heart Center. A donation that Abramovich made to Keren Kayemet Lelsrael Jewish National Fund for a comprehensive forest rehabilitation program in Israel's southern Negev desert, helps to combat the area's rising desertification and promotes increasing nature tourism to the area. Alongside his philanthropic activity, Abramovich has invested some $120 million in 20 Israeli start-ups, ranging from medicine and renewable energy to social media.

RECENTLY, DUE TO THE ALARMING INCREASE in COVID-19 cases in Israel, Abramovich gave Sheba Hospital another donation for a new subterranean Intensive Care Unit, spanning 5,400 square meters, to provide Israel with vital crisis response in times of national emergencies. Abramovich continuously contributes to Jewish art and culture initiatives, such as the M.ART contemporary culture festival in Tel Aviv, Israel.

ABRAMOVICH FILED AN APPLICATION FOR A residence permit in the canton of Valais, Switzerland in July 2016, a tax-friendly home to successful businessmen, and planned to transfer his tax residency to the Swiss municipality. Valais authorities readily agreed to the request and transferred the application to the Swiss State Secretariat for Migration for approval. Once there, FedPol investigators expressed suspicions and opposed the request. As a result, Abramovich withdrew his application in June 2017. After a tree-year legal saga, in 2021, Swiss authorities cleared Abramovich any suspicion.

IN APRIL 2021, ABRAMOVICH BECAME A Portuguese citizen as part of the country's Nationality Act; his genealogy was vetted by experts who look for "evidence of interest in Sephardic (Jewish) culture." Though *Reuters* noted that there is little known history of Sephardi Jews in Russia, Abramovich had donated money to projects honoring the legacy of Portuguese Sephardi Jews in Hamburg, Germany. However, on March 11, 2022, the leader of the Jewish Community in Porto, Rabbi Daniel Litvak, was arrested by Portuguese police at Porto airport amid allegations that certification of Sephardi Jewish origin had been issued corruptly in several cases. The allegations were later dropped for lack of evidence, with the judges criticizing the behavior of the prosecutors and of law enforcement, and saying all the allegations were 'generalities.

According to *Forbes*, as of March 2016, Abramovich had a net worth of US$7.6 billion, ranking him as the 155th richest person in the world. Prior to the 2008 financial crisis, he was considered to be the second richest person living within the United Kingdom. Early in 2009, *The Times* estimated that due to the global economic crisis, he had lost 3 billion British pounds from his 11.7 billion wealth. In the summer of 2020, Abramovich sold the gold mine Highland Gold to Vladislav Sviblov. On March 5, 2021, *Forbes* listed his net worth at US$14.5 billion, ranking him 113 on the Billionaires 2020 Forbes list.

FIVE

OKAY, THAT'S THE ABRAMOVICH STORY, so far, but it doesn't end there. It seems that after hearing from his brother in New York—all about what it's like to live in a place where you can do just about anything you want to do—Abramovich decided that being one of the world's richest men wasn't what he really wanted. He knew he was taking a huge risk and that Vladimir Putin wouldn't like it, but he decided to go ahead, anyway.

He asked for a meeting with his lawyer, Pyotr Alexandrovich Mushin, and directed him to make a list of four clinics in downtown Moscow: Zelenograd, Mytishi, Lubertsy, and Vidnoye

The Zelenograd clinic was reserved for dependents (wives and children) of Russian soldiers killed in Ukraine. At last count there were 1,340 of them and the list was growing each day.

The Mytishi clinic was reserved for orphans whose parents had either divorced or, in most cases, their fathers had died in Ukraine.

The Lubertsy clinic was the largest of the four, accepting patients of all ages and sexes, mostly drug addicts and teen age members some of Moscow's street gangs.

Vidnoye was the smallest of the four, accepting only those patients who were either too poor or too sick to function in the real world.

Lawyer Mushin asked his client how much he should give to each of the four named recipients. Answer: as much as they say they need and do it so that it's exempt from taxation.

Then, his nearly unbelievable request: Ask for a visitor's visa to the United States, figuring that once there he could stay with his brother.

BACK TO OUR STORY.

"We'll get to that later. For now we agree that Natasha should go to Tashkent, (she was born there, you may recall) renew old friendships and ask some hard questions of the authorities. Uzbekistan is an independent nation now, no longer one of the Soviet Union's fifteen republics. As you know, we have an embassy there, a small consular staff and, as I understand it, our ambassador there is on good terms with the local leadership."

"Yes, Robert, that's true. And I know the man, David Rostov. His grandparents were born in Leningrad, they survived Stalin's reign and made their way to Finland. David's parents wanted to settle in Moscow—this was when Nikita Khruschev was in charge—and they decided to ask for United States' citizenship. Now, both his parents an David himself, have that so-called Green Card, meaning that in five years—or less—they'll be citizens. And the State Department had to fudge the rules a bit, to make a green card holder one of its staff.

"But you'll like David. His wife was born in Brooklyn, New York, grew up in one of those Russian-speaking ghettos, took an ESL course and now she speaks both Russian and English."

"Children?"

"No, insofar as I know.

Aeroflot's Boeing 777's flight to Tashkent was on time, four hours after leaving Moscow's Vnukovo airport. With their diplomatic passports in hand, the couple moved directly to baggage claim and from their to the embassy's waiting Lada four-door sedan. Its driver introduced himself as Sergey Romanovich Borisov, and explained that the drive to the Tashkent embassy would take only twenty minutes. Oxner thought this a good time to start a friendly conversation with Sergey and, although he already knew the answer, he asked it anyway.

"What do you know about that terrible earthquake, Sergey?"

"Well, Sir, that was nearly 60 years ago, but it was really bad. April 26, 1966, with a 5.2 magnitude. Many of the buildings were completely destroyed, flights in and out of the city were canceled, and as I understand, it took about five years for the city to rebuild itself. I don't think anybody knows how many people died and with the hospitals badly damaged—well, it was just awful. Fortunately, there aren't many people still living who remember those days."

Twenty minutes later, in ambassador Rostov's office.

"So, at last we meet, and welcome to Tashkent. I understand that you, Natasha, were born and grew up here."

"That's true Mr. ambassador. And I'm still able to speak Uzbek, although poorly because I have no need to use it. But Robert and I can converse in either Russian or English and that makes it much easier."

"Yes, I should think so. So, tell me, Robert, what brings you and your wife to Tashkent? The messages I've been receiving from both Washington and Moscow seem to be deliberately vague about this."

"That's not an accident, Sir. What this visit is about is to learn what you're able to tell us about any kind of jihadist revival. Even though it's been many years since that Seal Team Six killed bin

Laden, we're concerned that there probably is some effort to bring his terrorist movement back into being."

"Yes. You're right about that. We have a liaison officer who meets regularly with the chief of the SSS, the State Security Service, Rahim Abdul Khazan. And his service has identified three men whom we believe have formed a kind of super-secret cell. These are devout Muslims, of course, and they feel obliged to follow Prophet Muhammad's instructions to kill those infidels who refuse to believe in what the Qur'an teaches."

"If you can give us the names of these people, plus any other identifying information, we can ask CIA headquarters to run traces on these three."

"Okay, here are the names we have:

Ali Azam, Abdullah Bashir and Zayan Abdi.

Azam's DPOB: 10/9/93, Cairo;

Bashir: 8/15/89, Cairo; at age 35, he's the oldest of the three.

Abdi: 6/13/94, Damascus.

"I should add that each of these guys is a Shi'ah Muslim, not Sunni. So one can assume that they get along with each other. And, as far as we know, each of them is still single, no wives or kids to worry about.

"SO, HERE ARE THE TRACES, JUST in from CIA Headquarters:

Ali Azam, DPOB 10/9/93, Cairo. Azam got a degree in Islamic history from Cairo University. He's a committed jihadist and brags about it. Most recent info about him tells us he has recruited three like-minded Egyptians and they are planning to hold rallies in downtown Cairo, urging their listeners to help them overthrow the Egyptian government.

Abdullah Bashir is a Kuwaiti citizen. His wife Carmella is a 35-year-old fashion model who displays the latest women's apparel, most of it imported from the United States.

Zayan Abdi is a stay-at-home homosexual who has never married but who has several male friends of about the same age, with whom he meets each Friday after religious services, in his home, where they "pleasure" each other.

"Okay, enough of that. Now, I should insert a piece I wrote some time ago about the Muslim Brotherhood. This will remind anyone who reads it that the Brotherhood's history is worth knowing."

THE MUSLIM BROTHERHOOD IS EGYPT'S OLDEST and largest Islamist organization with offshoots throughout the Arab world. The Brotherhood renounced violence in the 1970s and earned popular support by providing social services such s pharmacies, hospitals and schools.

After the ouster of former president Hosni Mubarak in the Arab Spring protests of 2011, the group's political arm won a plurality of seats in Egypt's lower house of parliament and its candidate Muhammad Morsi, was elected president. But Morsi was ousted by the military in July 2013 and the Brotherhood's were imprisoned, went into exile or were forced underground. As part of a wide-ranging crackdown on political opposition, the Egyptian government has labeled the group a terrorist organization, as have Saudi Arabia, and the United Arab Emirates. U.S. president Donald Trump has expressed interest in following suit, but many experts say a designation—whether of the original Egyptian group or of kindred groups throughout the region—would stretch the bounds of law and also complicate U.S. diplomacy across much of the Middle East and North Africa.

Founded in 1928 by Hasan al-Banna, the Muslim Brotherhood is the world's most influential Islamist organization. The Brotherhood's mission is to Islamize society through the promotion of religious law, values, and morals. It has long combined preaching and political activism with social welfare to advance this objective.

The group earned legitimacy among its core constituency, the lower middle class, as the most effective organized resistance against the British occupation of Egypt (1882 – 1952). The Brotherhood joined with the Free Officers, nationalist military leaders who sought to wrest Egypt from a British-backed monarchy. After a coup d'etat that forced King Farouk out of power in July 1952, the military junta that took charge and the Brotherhood became rivals. This conflict was over power and ideology; the Brotherhood rejected the military's vision of Egypt as the leader of a socialist, secular, and pan-Arab movement.

In 1954, a suspected member of the Brotherhood attempted to assassinate the leader of the Free Officers, Gamal Abdel Nasser. In response, thousands of suspected Brothers were imprisoned. Though Nasser barred the group from government, the Brotherhood nevertheless became ubiquitous in society, building allegiance as a populist alternative to the Egyptian state, which provided neither prosperity nor welfare and suffered repeated military defeats by Israel.

Among those arrested was a member of the Brotherhood named Sayyid Qutb, who developed a doctrine of armed struggle against the regime in Egypt and beyond, while writing from prison. His work has provided the underpinnings for many Sunni Islamist groups, including al-Qaeda and Hamas. Extremist leaders often cite Qutb, who was hanged in 1966, to argue that governments not based on sharia are apostate and therefor legitimate targets of jihad.

Though establishing a state based on Islamic principles was at the core of the Brotherhood's agenda, the group gained prominence by effectively providing social services where the state failed.

The Brotherhood renounced violence at the insistence of Nasser's successor, Anwar al-Sadat, who allowed the group to preach and advocate in exchange for it support against political rivals, Nasser loyalists, and leftists. Sadat paid lip service in sharia and freed imprisoned Islamists. He was assassinated in 1981 by members of al-Jihad, an extremist group whose leaders opposed Sadat's 1979 peace treaty with Israel—though they were not the only ones—and sought the violent overthrow of the Egyptian political system because it was not based on religious law.

Although Egypt was not a democracy, it did hold parliamentary elections. Brotherhood-affiliated candidates first participated in parliamentary elections in 1984, even as the party remained banned. An alliance with the officially-recognized Wafd Party, which stood for nationalism and economic liberalism, won 65 of the parliament's 450 seats. Running as independents in the early 2000s, Brotherhood candidates won still more seats, forming the largest opposition bloc.

The Brotherhood emerged as a dominant political force in Egypt following Mubarak's removal from office amid mass protests in February 2011. The Brotherhood's organizational capacity was unmatched, but the group's electoral victories were tarnished by power struggles with the judiciary and the military. Battles over the drafting of a new constitution were a particular flash point.

In the 2012 parliamentary elections, the Brotherhood's Freedom and Justice party won nearly half the seats in the lower house and Islamists took 84 percent of the seats in the upper house (Shura Council.) Pushing back against the Brotherhood's increasing power, the Mubarak-appointed Supreme Constitutional Court issued a decision in June 2012 that led to the dissolution of the People's Assembly. At the same time, the Supreme Council of the Armed Forces, which had been in control of Egypt since Mubarak's fall, gave the miliary exclusive control over defense and national security, diminishing the power of the president.

Just before Mubarak had stepped aside, the Brotherhood said that it would not seek the presidency, but it nevertheless put forward Khairat el-Shater, the deputy spiritual head, as a candidate. After he was disqualified, Morsi took his place. In a contest that posed a choice between Ahmad Shafiq—who had been a government minister during the Mubarak years and briefly prime minister after the January 2011 uprising— and the Brotherhood's candidate, Morsi was announced the winner in June 2012.

With the lower house of parliament dissolved, Morsi had both executive and legislative control of the government. In late November 2012, he declared himself, the Shura Council and the constituent assembly immune from judicial review. Morsi had justified the move by arguing that the judiciary and much of the bureaucracy was dominated by remnants of the Mubarak regime intent on impeding the revolution's goals. But after an immediate backlash, including public demonstrations, he annulled the decree.

The new constitution, which enshrined Islamic law as the basis for legislation, also stirred controversy. Though a similar principle existed in Egypt's prior constitution, the new draft raised concern with Egyptian liberals suspicious that the Brotherhood would take it as license to codify its worldview in the law. Many Egyptians also feared insufficient protections for women's rights and freedoms of speech and worship and distrusted the broad power accorded to the presidency. The constitution was approved with a 64 percent majority in a nationwide referendum, but only a third of the electorate voted.

The conflict between Morsi and the judiciary continued in March 2013, when the Supreme Administrative Court overturned a presidential decree calling for April parliamentary elections, questioning the constitutionality of election law provisions. The secular opposition had previously called for a boycott of the vote.

Many analysts criticized Morsi's tactics as majoritarian, and Egyptians critical of the Brotherhood coalesced around the group Tamarrod (Rebellion) which claimed to gather twenty-two million signatories to a petition calling for Morsi to step down. As the Tamarrod movement gained steam, Egyptians complained of a breakdown in security and about Brotherhood vigilantism. Bringing things to a head, Morsi appointed a member of the former militant group Jamaat al-Islamiyya as governor of Luxor, where the group had massacred dozens of tourists in 1997.

As millions of protestors amassed in the streets, the Supreme Council of the Armed Forces—the same body that had forced Mubarak aside—issued ultimatum to Morsi, giving him forty-eight hours to meet their demands. On July 3, 2013, SCAF, led by Defense Minister Abdel Fatah al-Sisi, ousted Morsi and suspended the new constitution.

The following month, security forces responded harshly to sit-ins protesting the coup, killing more than

1,150 demonstrators. Human Rights Watch found. The main encampment, Rabaa al-Adawiya Square, became a rallying cry for opposition to the new regime.

THE GOVERNMENT OUTLAWED THE MUSLIM BROTHER-HOOD, forcing it underground once again. Under Sisi, who became president in May 2014, the regime has taken strong steps to repress any opposition, using accusations of membership in the Brotherhood to repress dissent of all stripes.

Thousands of the group's leaders have been imprisoned, and others went into exile. The group's charities have been shuttered and their assets confiscated. Morsi, who has been on trial ever since his ouster, died in June 2019 after being denied medical care while being held in solitary confinement, according to Human Rights Watch. It was the seventh anniversary of his election.

Unable to seek a voice through political or civic participation, some members of the Egyptian Muslim Brotherhood could split off into radical factions and resort to violence, analysts say. In this way the group could be forced in a direction far different than that of its offshoots, many of which have taken part in parliamentary politics as socially conservative parties.

Qatar and Turkey have cultivated ties with the Brotherhood, and many exiled members of the Egyptian group have settled in those countries. In contrast, Saudi Arabia and the UAE have worked to suppress Brotherhood-affiliated movements, seeking their populist appeal as an ideological rival to their absolute monarchies. They have advocated a broad-brush U.S. terrorist designation. That would treat disparate movements and parties around the region as if they were all part of a monolithic organization, when in reality the original Egyptian organization's influence over the diffuse network has been diminished, officials and experts say.

"Hmm, That's quite a story, most of which I knew nothing about. But, we need to move on. And by the way, it's been confirmed that Abramovich is now living in New York and helping his brother. He has a green card and in five years will become a United States citizen.

EPILOGUE

1 400 HOURS, CRIMEA, IN SEVASTOPOL'S COMMUNITY Clinic's library. One of its male nurses is reading a day-old copy of one of Moscow's newspapers.

"A few Western governments have decided to hit Russian president Vladimir Putin where it might hurt: in Western safe havens where they keep and spend their money.

"Late last month, U.S. and U.K. officials said they were preparing economic sanctions for possible use against both sectors of the Russian economy as well as wealthy Russian individuals with close connections to Russian president Vladimir Putin and senior Russian government officials. The measures could include family members of the targeted people.

"Sanctions would cut them off from the international financial system and ensure that they and their family members will no longer be able to enjoy the perks of parking their money in the West and attending elite

Western universities, a senior U.S. official told *Reuters* late last month. The sanctions regime that U.K. officials say they are devising may be the most worrying for rich Russians, who have long seen London as a safe destination for storing and growing their wealth."

"HMM, THAT'S NOT GOOD NEWS FOR our latest patient, who just happens to be the man this article is about, Vladimir Putin. His granddaughter Maria will be here any moment and I have to believe she's also read this piece. Yes, she just walked in."

"Maria, have you seen this?"

"Yes, I read it as soon as I got off the plane. Awful, isn't it?"

"The more important question is whether your grandfather has read it. You can ask him; he's sitting in that wheelchair on the patio."

"GRANDPA! IT'S SO GOOD TO SEE you again!"

"Ah, yes. Maria. How did you find me?"

"I called the Kremlin's switchboard and they told me you're here. How long do you plan to stay?"

"Unfortunately, I'm told I'm not going anywhere. They say I have lung cancer, too damned many cigarettes. I've tried to quit but it never worked. They tell me I'll likely be dead within a week or so."

"If that's true, Grandpa, how do you want to be remembered?"

"Come again."

"Okay, you know that many people—and not just Russians—think of you as one of the world's most evil men, because of your war in Ukraine and your unlawful annexation of Crimea.

"Plus the fact that many of your staff, especially mothers with children, have become drug addicts and are unable to perform their duties."

"Yes, I'm aware of that; but there's not much I can do about it."

"Forgive me, Grandpa, but that's not true. What you can do is tell your colleagues in the Kremlin to notify the Ukrainian authorities that you want to stop the killing and the war to end; and all the troops to go home. And you can do it right now, with my cell phone.

SO THE QUESTION REMAINS: will he or won't he?

JOHN SAGER IS A RETIRED United States Intelligence officer whose services for the CIA, in various capacities, spanned more than a half-century. A widower, he makes his home in the Covenant Shores retirement community, on Mercer Island, Washington.

Milton Keynes UK
Ingram Content Group UK Ltd.
UKHW050731031124
450591UK00024B/332